NICK BUTTERWORTH
THE WHISPERER

HarperCollins *Children's Books*

Cats fighting. I love it!
I mean, when they're
fighting each other, they're
not coming after me, see?
or my kind.

My kind? Well, you could say
we're a bit like mice.

OK, a little bigger. But just
as cuddly. I'm a rat.

Hey! Don't go. Listen up.
I've got a story
for you . . .

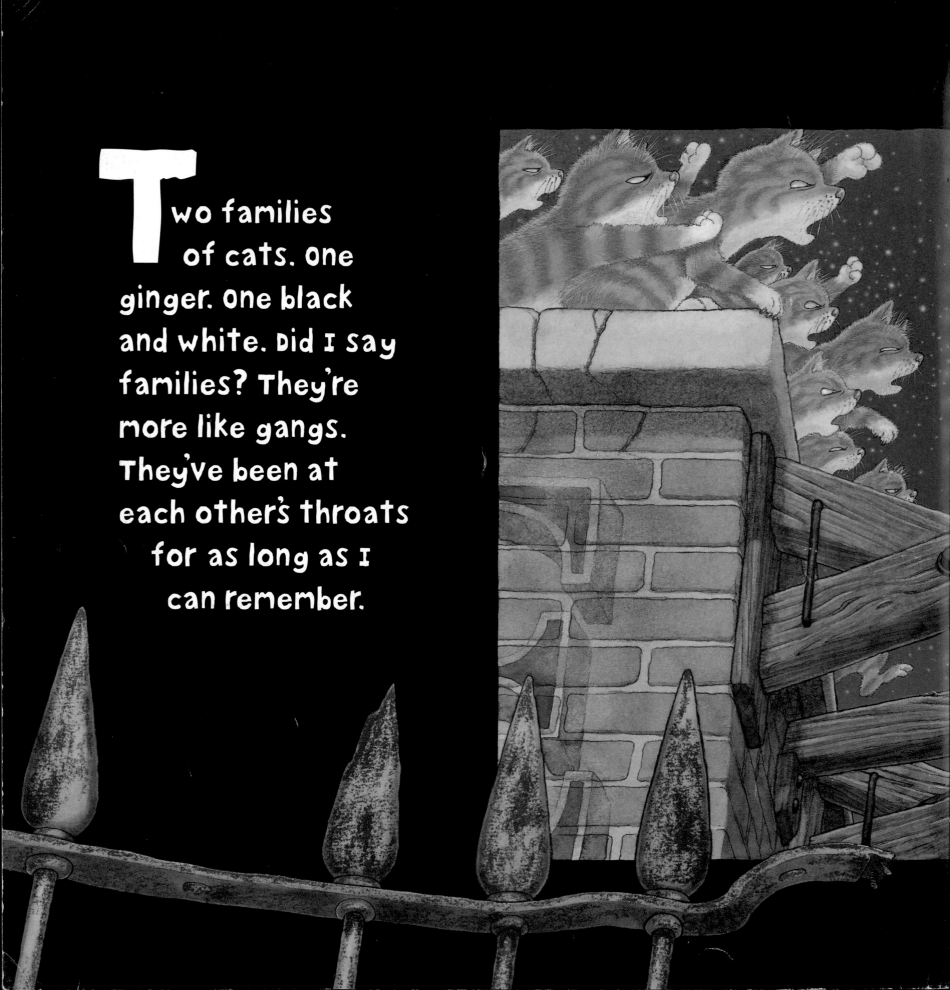

Two families
of cats. One
ginger. One black
and white. Did I say
families? They're
more like gangs.
They've been at
each other's throats
for as long as I
can remember.

They're rude. They spit. They call each other terrible names. And they fight like . . . well, like cats. All the time. So.

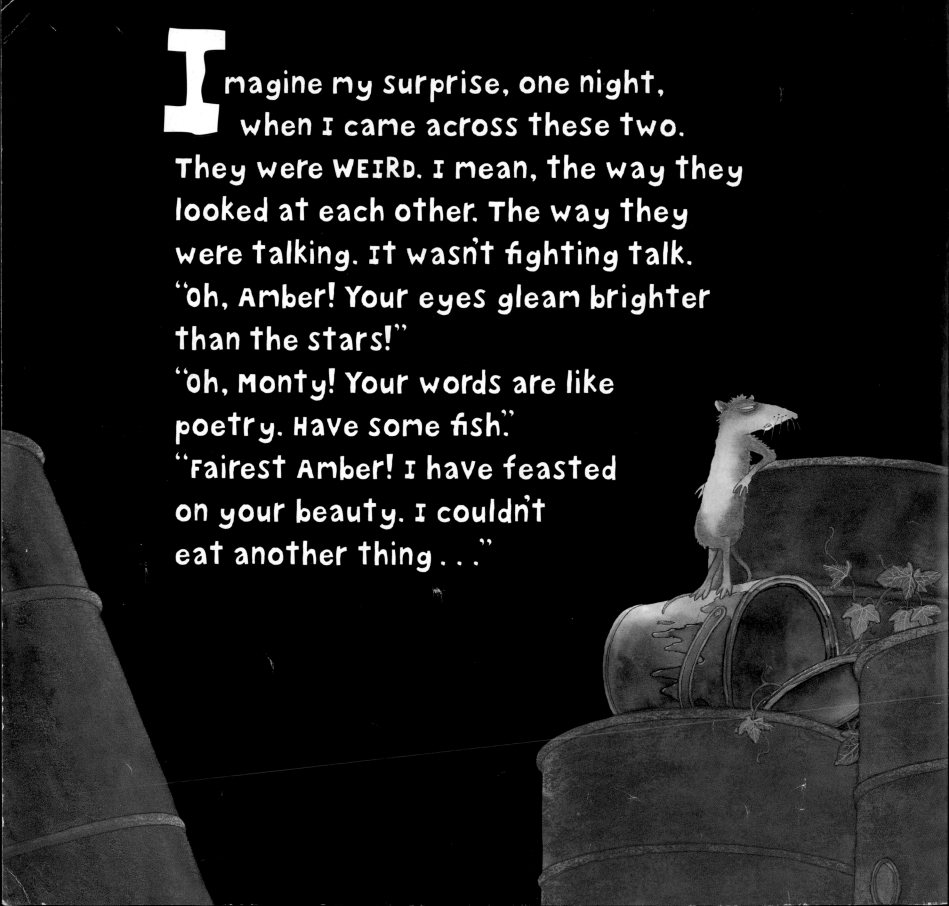

Imagine my surprise, one night,
when I came across these two.
They were WEIRD. I mean, the way they
looked at each other. The way they
were talking. It wasn't fighting talk.
"Oh, Amber! Your eyes gleam brighter
than the stars!"
"Oh, Monty! Your words are like
poetry. Have some fish."
"Fairest Amber! I have feasted
on your beauty. I couldn't
eat another thing . . ."

Stars . . . poetry . . . fish . . . what was all that about? What'd got into them? Suddenly I knew. It was **LOVE!** Oh, Amber! Oh, Monty! Oh, Yeeeuch!

This was bad. These two were the son and daughter of the rival gang leaders. The gangs would have to be told. Just one problem . . . how?

There was only one way. The whisper. It's the best. Better than shouting. Better than a letter. Better than anything. Everybody hears the whisper . . .

. . . but they don't see the whisperer! It's beautiful. I began to whisper. Through drain pipes. Through thin walls. Into all the right ears. My whisper ran wild!

It worked! The gang leaders called an Emergency Truce. For just one hour they agreed to stop all fighting, so they could deal with this **LOVE** business.
The **LOVE CATS** were made to stand before the gangs. Old Ginger Tom spoke first.
He was serious.

"This is a disgrace," he said. "You have betrayed yourselves, and your families." Then, up spoke One-Eyed Flossie. "I hate to do it," she said, "but I have to agree with this old fleabag. Now you must choose. Go back to your families. See each other no more, and we'll forget all about this dreadful business . . ."

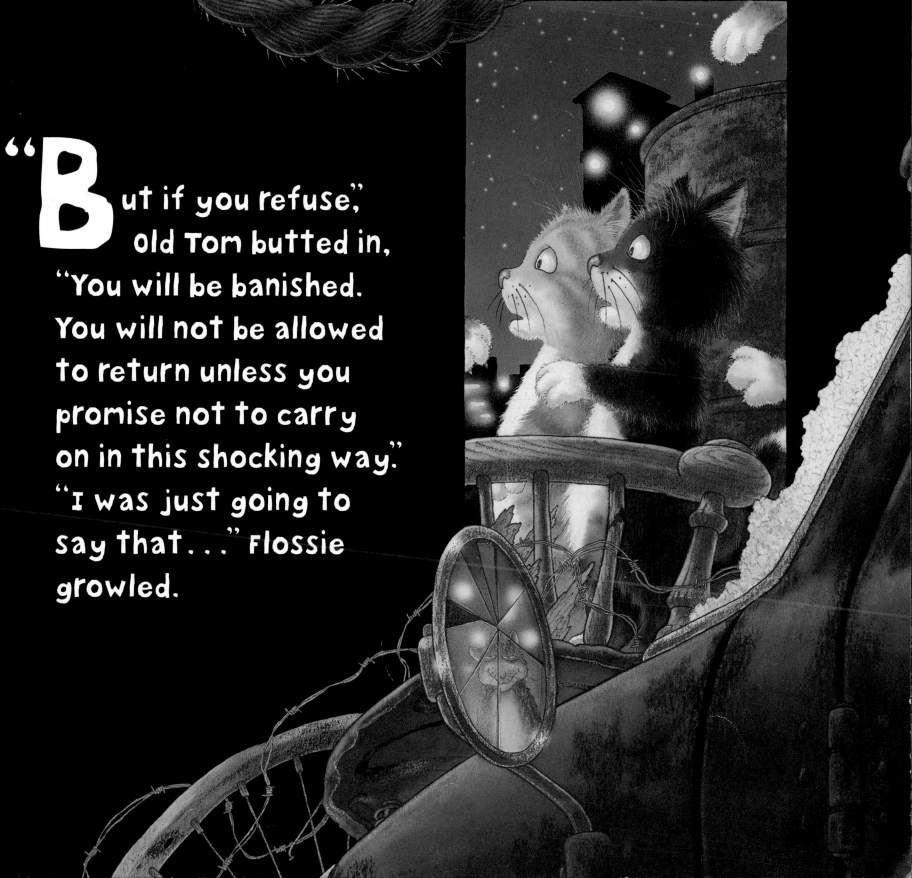

"**B**ut if you refuse," old Tom butted in, "You will be banished. You will not be allowed to return unless you promise not to carry on in this shocking way." "I was just going to say that . . ." Flossie growled.

"This is just too hard," Amber said.
Her voice was all wobbly. Like she
was going to cry. Hee, hee!

"We can't do it," said Monty. "If we must
choose . . . We choose to go."
Yes! Oh, yes! Hip Hip Hooray! Goodbye, my
lovey-dovey friends! And GOOD RIDDANCE.

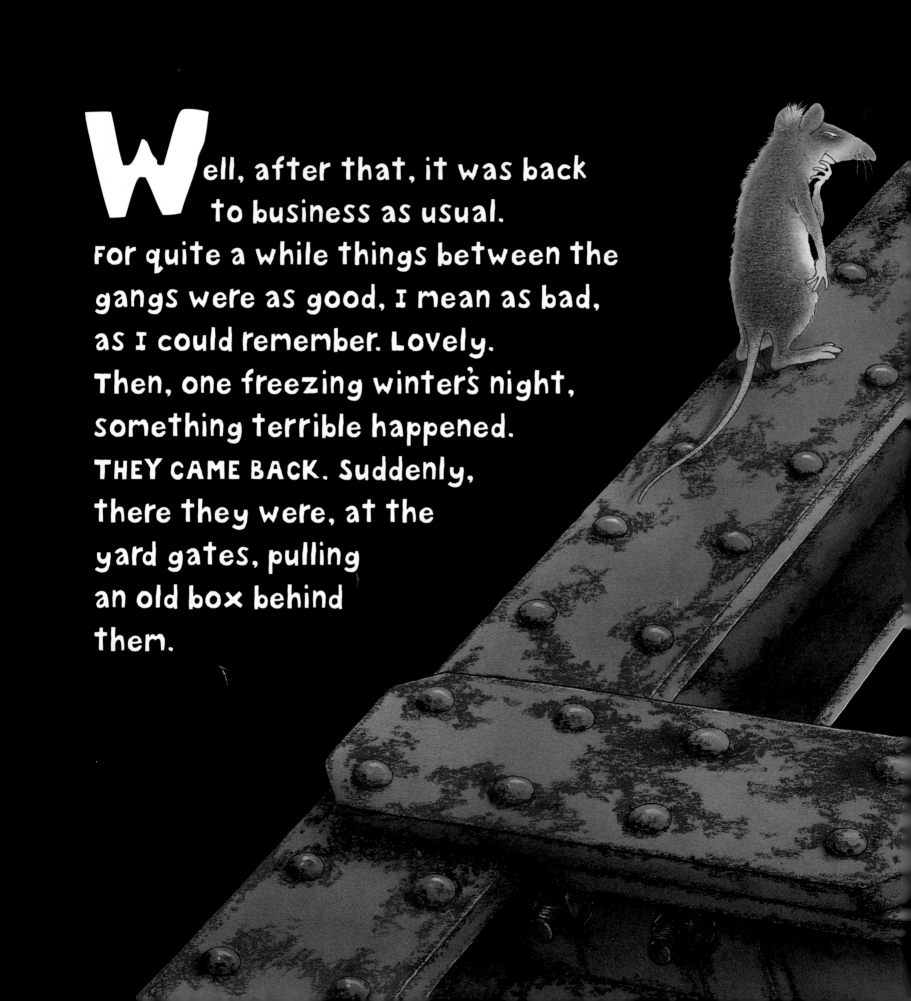

Well, after that, it was back to business as usual.
For quite a while things between the gangs were as good, I mean as bad, as I could remember. Lovely.
Then, one freezing winter's night, something terrible happened.
THEY CAME BACK. Suddenly, there they were, at the yard gates, pulling an old box behind them.

Straight away, the two of them were surrounded by cats. Hissing. Murmuring. Old Tom and Flossie pushed their way through. "We take it", Flossie purred, "you have come back because you realise you need your families. Good."

Then she snapped, "Now you must separate. Go back to your families. Hang your heads in shame."

"We do need our families," said Monty. "But, before you force us to separate, there is something you should see."

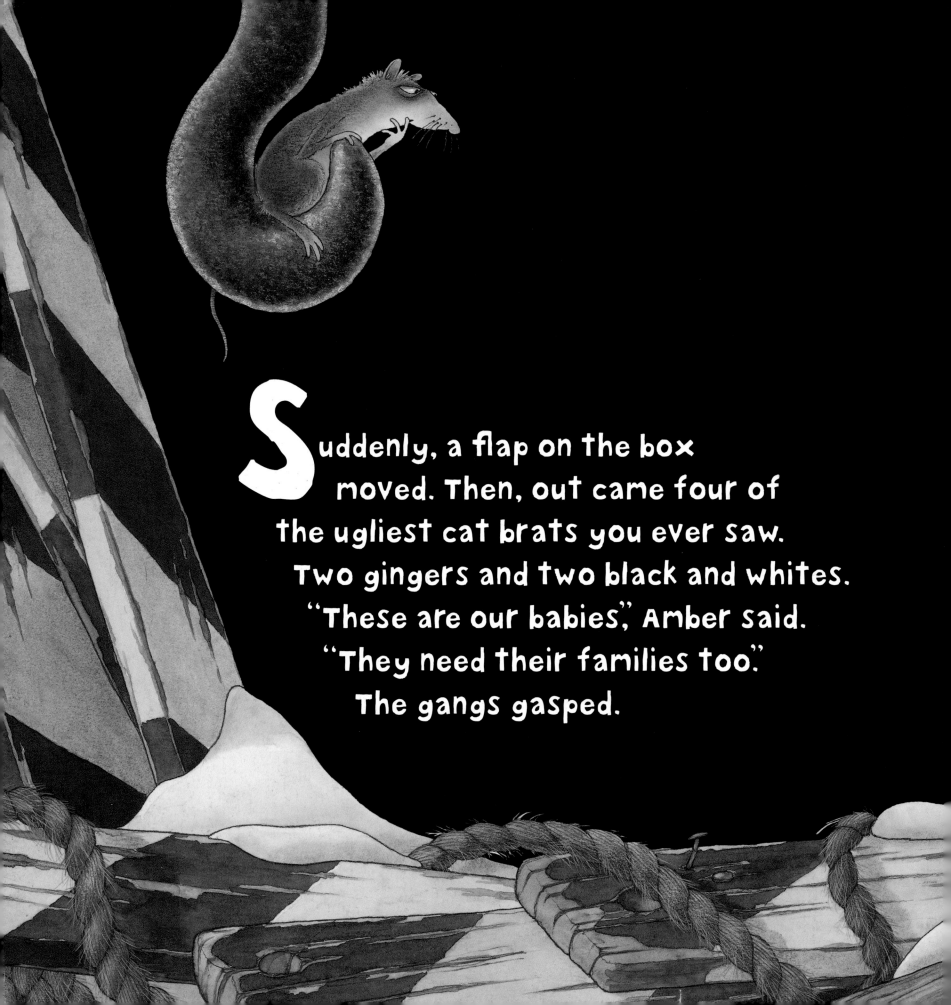

Suddenly, a flap on the box
moved. Then, out came four of
the ugliest cat brats you ever saw.
Two gingers and two black and whites.
"These are our babies," Amber said.
"They need their families too."
The gangs gasped.

Old Tom smiled. But he wasn't laughing. "This is no problem," he said. "These little beauties will go to their mother's family with her . . .

And these, these, black and
white MOGGIES will go
with their father to HIS lot.
That's easily settled."

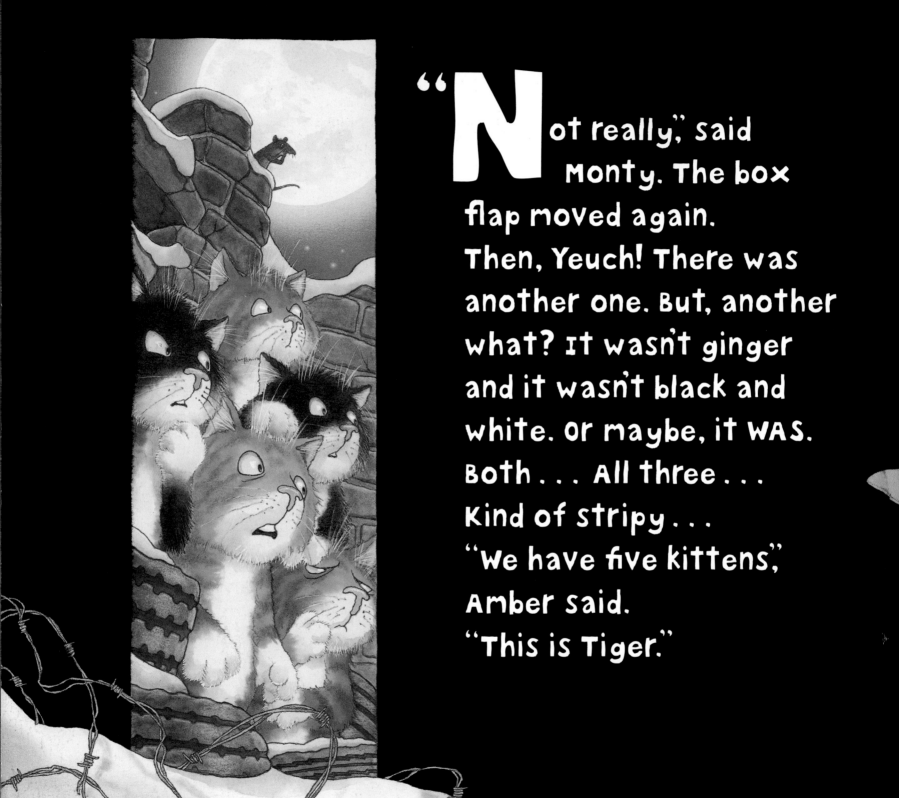

"Not really", said Monty. The box flap moved again. Then, Yeuch! There was another one. But, another what? It wasn't ginger and it wasn't black and white. Or maybe, it WAS. Both... All three... Kind of stripy...

"We have five kittens", Amber said.

"This is Tiger."

It was the first time I've ever seen
Flossie or Old Tom lost for words.
Speechless, they were.
Amber picked up the one she called
Tiger and held him close to them both.
"Say 'hello' to your Gran and Grandad,
Tiger," she said.

I'm worried. They've called a truce while they sort out this Tiger business. What if they get used to NOT fighting? Or worse, what if they come after me? And my kind . . . NO. Those dumb old cats won't change. I'll lie low. I'll get whispering. I'll be fine . . . don't you think?

But what about those, CAT BRATS? I've got a bad feeling about them. If they get on to me . . . hey . . .

I'm gone.

Dedicated to
Archbishop Desmond Tutu...
a pussy-cat and a tiger!
N.B.

First published in hardback in Great Britain by HarperCollins Children's Books in 2004

1 3 5 7 9 10 8 6 4 2

ISBN: 0-00-712017-6

HarperCollins Children's Books is a division of HarperCollins Publishers Ltd.

Text and illustrations copyright © Nick Butterworth 2004

Visit our website at: www.harpercollinschildrensbooks.co.uk

Printed and bound in Singapore